Cat & Cat

PAPERCUTZ

MORE GREAT GRAPHIC NOVEL SERIES AVAILABLE FROM
PAPERCUTZ™

THE SMURFS

ASTERIX

DANCE CLASS

THE SISTERS

CAT & CAT

GERONIMO STILTON

GERONIMO STILTON REPORTER

MELOWY

DINOSAUR EXPLORERS

ATTACK OF THE STUFF

THE MYTHICS

FUZZY BASEBALL

THE RED SHOES

THE LITTLE MERMAID

BLUEBEARD

HOTEL TRANSYLVANIA

THE LOUD HOUSE

GUMBY

THE ONLY LIVING BOY

THE ONLY LIVING GIRL

Go to papercutz.com for more information
Also available where ebooks are sold.

2. CAT OUT OF WATER

CHRISTOPHE CAZENOVE
HERVÉ RICHEZ
SCRIPT

YRGANE RAMON
ART

PAPERCUTZ
New York

To my parents,

To Kali, Patate & Pitou, Toudougras,
To Qwerty & Crokopik,

To Pioute, Eliott & Ness, Lola, the little keg, Mimi38,
To Croustiflette, Verveine, Tortue Géniale, Baboin, Symétrie, Igloo, Moquette, Sablier, Faux-filet, Capuchon, and
all the other cats I renamed in my town, from not knowing their real names.
To Bamboo, Timmy, Tyrion, June, Arwen, Mya, Lily, Socket & Cendre, Canaillou, the ferret with positive waves.
To every gang of purrers, to all loving heasties.
To those who look after animals.
To the late Kiki, my rabbit, who crunched his last dandelion bloom this year.
To Sarujin & Olivier Plazas for their prepping help for colorization for this book.
To the friends & readers who bring life to this series.
Thanks to SaruJin & Olivier Plazas for their prep work help for colorization of this book.
Thanks!
– Yrgane
www.yrgane.com

And always to Céline…
– Hervé

Cat & Cat

#2 "Cat Out of Water"
Christophe Cazenove &
Hervé Richez – Writers
Yrgane Ramon – Artist
Joe Johnson – Translator
Wilson Ramos Jr. – Letterer

Special thanks to Catherine Loiselet

Production – Mark McNabb
Editor – Ellen S. Abramowitz
Managing Editor – Jeff Whitman
Editorial Intern – Eric Storms
Jim Salicrup
Editor-in-Chief

Papercutz books may be purchased for business or promotional use. For information on bulk purchases
please contact Macmillan Corporate and Premium Sales Department at (800) 221-795 x5442.

Hardcover ISBN: 978-1-5458-0478-0
Paperback ISBN: 978-1-5458-0479-7

Printed in Lithuania
July 2020

Distributed by Macmillan
First Papercutz Printing

5

11

21

27

37

43

53

55

56

58

59

I really do live with strange people... That thing there, full of water, what's it really for?

It's not a water bowl. It's too big and the water smells weird!

Maybe it's an aquarium! Uh, well no, there aren't any fish!

A bathtub? A sink for the dishes? Unless...

WHY, YES!

I got it!

Okay, it's not for COOKING food either...

65

They sleep all the time... Their fur is all puffy... So, you suddenly got to stop brushing them...

They eat twice as much hard food! The short time they're awake, you have to spend your time serving them...

Uh... you're taking Sushi to sleep with you, now?

Oh, yes! Cats are super useful in the winter!

MMMM! NITEY-NITE!

75

78

81

84

87

88

89

WATCH OUT FOR PAPERCUTZ

Welcome to the second washed up graphic novel of CAT AND CAT, by Christophe Cazenove and Hervé Richez, writers, and Yrgane Ramon, artist, from Papercutz, those crazy cat-video connoisseurs dedicated to publishing great graphic novels for all ages. I'm Jim Salicrup, the Editor-in-Chief and Keeper of the Kitty Litter. In CAT AND CAT #1 (which is still available at libraries and booksellers everywhere), I told you how cat-crazy we are at Papercutz and listed many of the Papercutz graphic novels that featured our favorite felines. Well, in the interest of equal time for canines, we wanted to mention there's an absolutely adorable little doggie in an exciting new series available from Papercutz right now. The dog's name is Dogmatix, and the series is called ASTERIX. It's a really big deal that Papercutz is publishing it, as ASTERIX is one of the biggest-selling graphic novel series in the world. This was big news and was even reported in *The New York Times* and *The Hollywood Reporter*. But regarding Dogmatix, while he does appear briefly—for one whole panel—in ASTERIX #1, it isn't until ASTERIX #2, where he starts to play a bigger role in the series.

Now some of you may not have heard of this Asterix fella, so let's take a quick journey in the Papercutz time machine...

We're back in the year 50 BC in the ancient country of Gaul, located where France, Belgium, and the Southern Netherlands are today. All of Gaul has been conquered by the Romans... well, not all of it. One tiny village, inhabited by indomitable Gauls, resists the invaders again and again. That doesn't make it easy for the garrisons of Roman soldiers surrounding the village in fortified camps.

So, how's it possible that a small village can hold its own against the mighty Roman Empire? The answer is this guy...

This is **Asterix**. A shrewd, little warrior of keen intellect... and superhuman strength. Asterix gets his superhuman strength from a magic potion. But he's not alone.

Obelix is Asterix's inseparable friend. He too has superhuman strength. He's a menhir (tall, upright stone monuments) deliveryman, he loves eating wild boar and getting into brawls. Obelix is always ready to drop everything to go off on a new adventure with Asterix. His constant companion (starting with ASTERIX #2) is Dogmatix, the only known canine ecologist, who howls with despair when a tree is cut down.

Panoramix, the village's venerable Druid, gathers mistletoe and prepares magic potions. His greatest success is the power potion. When a villager drinks this magical elixir he or she is temporarily granted super-strength. This is just one of the Druid's potions! And now you know why this small village can survive, despite seemingly impossible odds.

It's time we get back to the palatial Papercutz offices and wrap this up. Now, where did we park our time machine? Oh, there it is!

We're back. Of course, you may find dogs in other Papercutz titles — Charles in THE LOUD HOUSE and Puppy in THE SMURFS, for just a couple examples — but we're so excited about ASTERIX, we couldn't resist sharing the news with you.

And if you still consider yourself more of a cat person and love Sushi (the cat, not the food), be sure not to miss the next CAT AND CAT graphic novel coming your way soon.

Thanks, *Jim*

STAY IN TOUCH!

EMAIL: salicrup@papercutz.com
WEB: www.papercutz.com
TWITTER: @papercutzgn
INSTAGRAM: @papercutzgn
FACEBOOK: PAPERCUTZGRAPHICNOVELS
FANMAIL: Papercutz, 160 Broadway, Suite 700, East Wing, New York, NY 10038

SPECIAL PREVIEW OF Asterix #1